$\frac{98}{17}$

The Lost Ears
Phillida Gili

Julia MacRae Books

A division of Franklin Watts

FOR LUCY SEKERS

First published in Great Britain by
Julia MacRae Books
A division of Franklin Watts, 8 Cork Street, London W1X 2HA
and Franklin Watts Inc, 730 Fifth Avenue, New York 10019
Designed by Jonathan Gili. Phototypeset by Tradespools Ltd.
Printed in Great Britain by Sackville Press, Billericay, Essex.

Gili, Phillida   The lost ears,   I. Title   823´.914 [J]   PZ7
LC No. 80–85290   ISBN 0–86203–033–1   U.S. ISBN 0–531–04065–8

Once upon a time there lived
a teddy bear called Harry, who
was only two and a half inches
tall.

He lived in Oliver's pajama pocket, where he felt warm and comfortable. Nothing much ever seemed to happen to him, but he was extraordinarily well-read for a bear. Because he could never resist reading whatever book Oliver was absorbed in.

Harry became an expert in
farming, knights and castles,
dogs, birds, trains, ships, deep
sea diving and dinosaurs, among
many other things; but he did
long to read a story that looked
at life from a bear's point of view.
 Then one day something
completely unexpected
happened to him.

Every week, Oliver's pajamas were bundled up and thrown into the laundry basket.

But this time Harry was still inside the pocket.

A minute later he felt himself being pushed into a dark hole, and a door was slammed in his face. He swam in circles for what seemed like hours; the hot soapy water tasted disgusting.

Finally he was spun until he was dizzy and then the pajamas were hung out on the line, with Harry still in the pocket, feeling weary and waterlogged. He also felt extremely sick. As he dried out he became stronger, but also very cross indeed.

Oliver's mother found him
when she ironed the pocket.

But oh dear! When Harry
looked in the mirror he got
a terrible shock.

He had lost his ears.

When Oliver saw him he said, "That can't be Harry! He looks ridiculous!" And he put him away in a dark cupboard with other broken toys. Poor Harry thought his reading days were over forever.

But quite a long time later, the
cupboard door was opened by
an inquisitive little girl called
Lucy. "Oh look at this dear
little teddy!" she said to
herself. "Poor thing! All he
needs are new ears. I'll
make him some at once."

She made a beautiful pair
out of felt. Later she made him
a red jacket, a blue scarf,
and a hat for cold days.

When Oliver saw Harry again
he could hardly recognize him.
He felt ashamed that he'd been
so unkind, and he put Harry
gently back into his pocket,
where he lived happily ever after.

Every week, Oliver made a
point of bringing Harry books
from the library about bears,
which pleased him very much.